The ONCE UPON AMERICA® Series

A LONG WAY TO GO
A Story of Women's Right to Vote
by Zibby Oneal

HERO OVER HERE
A Story of World War I
by Kathleen V. Kudlinski

IT'S ONLY GOODBYE
An Immigrant Story
by Virginia T. Gross

THE DAY IT RAINED FOREVER
A Story of the Johnstown Flood
by Virginia T. Gross

PEARL HARBOR IS BURNING!
A Story of World War II
by Kathleen V. Kudlinski

CHILD STAR
When Talkies Came to Hollywood
by Lydia Weaver

FIRE!
The Beginnings of the Labor Movement
by Barbara Diamond Goldin

THE BITE OF THE GOLD BUG
A Story of the Alaskan Gold Rush
by Barthe DeClements

CLOSE TO HOME
A Story of the Polio Epidemic
by Lydia Weaver

NIGHT BIRD
A Story of the Seminole Indians
by Kathleen V. Kudlinski

Night Bird

A STORY OF THE SEMINOLE INDIANS

BY KATHLEEN V. KUDLINSKI

ILLUSTRATED BY JAMES WATLING

VIKING

JF
KUDL

Many thanks to Alison Richards, Ph.D., director of the Peabody Museum
at Yale University, and to Robert Dewar, Ph.D., chairman
of the Anthropology Department, University of Connecticut,
who read this text for background authenticity.

VIKING
Published by the Penguin Group
Penguin Books USA Inc., 375 Hudson Street, New York, New York 10014, U.S.A.
Penguin Books Ltd, 27 Wrights Lane, London W8 5TZ, England
Penguin Books Australia Ltd, Ringwood, Victoria, Australia
Penguin Books Canada Ltd, 10 Alcorn Avenue, Toronto, Ontario, Canada M4V 3B2
Penguin Books (N.Z.) Ltd, 182–190 Wairau Road, Auckland 10, New Zealand

Penguin Books Ltd, Registered Offices: Harmondsworth, Middlesex, England

First published in 1993 by Viking, a division of Penguin Books USA Inc.

1   3   5   7   9   10   8   6   4   2

Once Upon America® is a registered trademark of Viking Penguin,
a division of Penguin Books USA Inc.

LIBRARY OF CONGRESS CATALOGING-IN-PUBLICATION DATA
Kudlinski, Kathleen V.
Night Bird : a story of Seminole Indians / by Kathleen V. Kudlinski:
illustrated by James Watling.   p.   cm.—(Once upon America)
Summary: In 1840 Night Bird, whose clan of Seminole Indians is
fighting to preserve its traditional way of life in Florida, must
decide whether to seek land and an unknown future in distant Oklahoma.
ISBN 0-670-83157-3
1. Seminole Indians—Juvenile fiction. [1. Seminole Indians—
Fiction. 2. Indians of North America—Florida—Fiction.]
I. Watling, James, ill. II. Title. III. Series.
PZ7.K9486N1   1993 [Fic]—dc20   92-25935 CIP AC

For Hank, as always—
this and every book.
But for you,
I would not be a writer.

Contents

It was the middle of June in 1840, south of the place that would become Disney World. None of the Seminole Indian tribe knew that, of course. The land was simply their home, though not their first one. Their calendar was the sky, not a piece of paper. And the sky said it was time to hold the Green Corn ceremony.

Too Much Noise

Noise—too much noise—had chased Night Bird to the edge of the island. Before her, the light of a new day spread over the quiet swamps. Behind her, songs and arguments, chants and jokes, filled the little Seminole Indian village. Dogs barked and chickens cackled. Children laughed too loudly and mothers scolded. Men bragged to each other. Babies cried.

The warm voices of Night Bird's own family were lost among all the other strange voices. These are my people, Night Bird told herself.

In front of her lay the Everglades, calm and still and flat. As far as she could see, there were low little islands poking up through the swamp grass. Turtles, Night Bird thought. The hummock islands look like giant turtles sleeping in the sun! A dozen new canoe trails wandered through the sawgrass, all leading to the island she was on, the Otter clan's island.

She looked down at the line of canoes at the edge of the water. Perhaps she could borrow one and slip away for a few minutes. The nearest hummock held fields full of newly ripened corn and squash. The next one was the burying ground—a peaceful place. Will anyone notice? she wondered. Night Bird looked quickly behind her and gasped.

An old woman stood silently by her elbow. Her feet were as bare as Night Bird's. Her neck was hidden under string after string of blue beads.

"Grandmother! What are you doing here?" As soon as the words were out of her mouth Night Bird blushed. How could she have been so rude? And to Grandmother, the head of the whole Otter clan! She covered her face with her hands. "Excuse me," she pleaded.

The old woman laughed and grasped Night Bird's hands. "I'm hiding, too," she said. "I'm not used to so many people."

"But I thought there were many more Seminoles back in your day." Night Bird stopped. Why couldn't she say anything right?

Grandmother laughed again, but she didn't sound upset. "Night Bird," she said, "I don't know you well, but I think I'm going to like you. Help me down the bank."

Night Bird knew about Grandmother's broken leg, of course. It had happened on a hummock far to the east and she had had to stay there until it healed. It had kept her from making the trip to the last two Green Corn ceremonies. And it had left Night Bird's own mother in charge of the clan and all the teaching, too.

Their long, faded skirts brushed together as they climbed down the bank. New skirts! Night Bird remembered. We get to wear our new skirts at the ceremony! And maybe get a new string of beads, too. Night Bird looked at Grandmother's blue necklaces as the old woman sat down on a log. What did Grandmother do to earn all those beads? she wondered.

The old woman was rubbing her leg. Her long hair was graying, but she didn't wear it in a bun, like other women. It was tied at her neck like a young girl's. Like mine, Night Bird thought.

"So much was different when I was your age," Grandmother said slowly. "Back in my time." She smiled.

"Oh, tell me!" Night Bird knew this was what she should say, but she really meant it, too. This would be a good story to tell and retell to her little brothers and sisters later, when the nights grew long. She listened hard to remember the words and the tone of the tale.

"Long ago, when I was eleven, the Seminole lived in cabins with four walls and dirt floors."

"Your houses had walls?" Night Bird was shocked.

Grandmother nodded. "We lived far, far to the north, where all the land was dry and good for farming, but it was much cooler. We wore leather clothes and moccasins on our feet."

Night Bird looked down at her bare feet. She wiggled her toes. How strange to wear clothes on your feet! she thought.

"Water ran only in streams, and sometimes it was so cold that the water itself turned hard." Grandmother looked out on the vast Everglades. "It was easier to live there." She was quiet for so long that Night Bird knew she was dreaming of this far northern place.

"Was *your* grandmother head of the Otter clan then?" she said gently.

"Oh, yes. I was afraid of her because she was so important. You're not scared of me, are you?"

"N-no." How could Night Bird answer this the way Grandmother wanted? Grandmother *was* the head of the whole clan, after all. She knew more stories, more dance steps, more ceremonies, and more healing herbs than anyone else.

Grandmother was still looking at her. "Well, a little," Night Bird finally said.

Grandmother laughed. "Good. Then I'm doing something right."

"It's just that you are so smart!" Night Bird said.

"You learn as you live. You know how you are taught just to listen and watch instead of asking questions? You're old enough to have learned that you can find out whatever you really need to know that way, aren't you?"

Night Bird nodded. It was so hard to teach that to the little ones. Then, after a while, it became habit.

"I'm not so smart. I've just been listening and watching longer than anyone else in the village." She patted Night Bird's knee. "You are a good listener, too."

Night Bird smiled and looked out at the swamps. She tried to imagine dry land. She couldn't. "I heard my mother say that there were more Seminoles then."

"Oh, yes. Thousands and thousands," Grandmother said. Night Bird drew in her breath. "And there were more than a hundred Otters." That was even harder to imagine than dry ground.

"The Green Corn ceremonies were so huge that you couldn't begin to know everyone who came," Grandmother continued slowly.

Where did they all go? Night Bird wanted to ask. Watch and listen, she reminded herself.

Grandmother sat looking out over the Everglades for so long that Night Bird began to think she had fallen asleep. Finally the old woman shook her head.

"White men," she said. Her voice sounded hard and

cold. There was no laughter in her now. "They pushed us south and south and south again, always taking more of our land. And killing." She paused again. "I watched them kill my grandmother. My father. My sister. I can still hear their screams. And see the blood."

Stop! Night Bird wanted to cry. The story was too horrible already and she could tell it wasn't done. "Each time they came they burned the village where I lived. Each time I watched from the woods and ran south with what was left of my family. And my poor clan."

It was as if someone else were talking, someone very different from the woman who laughed so easily. This woman was bursting with hate.

"And now," she continued, "they're simply taking my people away. They take families, whole villages, entire clans. I don't know why. They can't want these miserable swamplands. But still the soldiers keep coming."

Night Bird tried not to breathe, not to hear, not to feel. She knew they were all hiding from the soldiers. That a hiding hole had to be ready for every family's children. That gathering together for this sacred ceremony was dangerous. But in all of her eleven years, she had never heard anyone talk about the killing. Not this way.

She looked away from her grandmother's angry eyes, out over the peaceful swamps. Suddenly she jumped to her feet. "Someone is coming!" she cried.

A Terrible
Silence

"Help me up, girl." Night Bird watched Grandmother's face go pale as she struggled to her feet. She held out a hand to help, but the old woman pushed it away. "Who's in that canoe?" Grandmother pointed to the small dot far beyond the near hummock.

They stood side by side, stiff with worry. The boat wandered this way and that, following the path of deepest water—closer, ever closer.

"It's not soldiers," Night Bird said. Grandmother let out a long hiss of relief. No danger. At least not yet. They looked at each other and smiled.

Night Bird turned back toward the Everglades and took a deep breath. If it wasn't an attack, it was more guests for the Green Corn ceremony. More people to fit into their tiny village!

Who are they? Night Bird wondered. Everyone they thought would come was already here. She shaded her eyes and looked into the distance. The father was standing, of course, pushing the canoe along with a long pole. There was a mother. And there was a girl, too!

"More Otters," Grandmother said. Her voice was thick with joy.

"I thought there were only seven Otters left." Night Bird was confused. Her mother had told her that they were the only ones now who knew how to arrange the grounds and lead the dancing. They alone had to teach all the other clans at the ceremonies. That was why remembering was so important. Remembering the dances, the stories, and the songs—the order of things.

A picture came into her mind. It was her earliest memory. She must have been three, she thought, and she had been sitting with her cousin in the sand by the new fire. They had been practicing the ribbon dance by moving dolls about on the ground the way older girls were supposed to move. Then, she remembered, they both had gotten up and someone had taught them their very first dance.

She stared at the canoe. "Grandmother, is that Little Mouse?" Her voice shook. It couldn't be. Her

cousin had been taken by soldiers. The whole family had been taken. Little Mouse had to be dead!

"I had heard they were still alive," Grandmother said, "and living with white farmers far to the north. I just didn't believe it." She shook her head slowly. "I must get the others!" The old woman turned and ran back toward the village. She was limping, Night Bird saw. But she was running anyway.

Night Bird wanted to run, too. She wanted to sing. Instead, she began to do the steps of the ribbon dance, slowly at first, then faster and faster across the sand. Her necklaces bounced and her skirts flew. Her heart was pounding so loudly she didn't even need rattles on her knees to make the dance feel right. Little Mouse was back!

"Da-ti! Wa-gi!" Night Bird rushed to her father and mother as they approached the bank. Sun sparkled on the blue beads hanging thick around her mother's neck and on her father's silver breastplate. The black feather on his turban made him look so tall, Night Bird thought. Tall and handsome. Night Bird stood still beside her parents.

At last the canoe landed. "Little Mouse!" Night Bird ran to her cousin. They looked at each other for a moment. Little Mouse was dressed strangely, in a sort of sack that covered her from her neck to ankles. But her laughing dark eyes were the same. They hugged tightly.

Night Bird tried to make herself calm inside. "You

grew up," she said. "You're pretty." Do *I* look that old? Night Bird wondered.

Little Mouse laughed. "You're much prettier than me, cousin. And taller!" Little Mouse made her face calm. It lasted only a moment. Then she had to grin. Then she frowned, but another grin broke right through. Her face looked so funny that Night Bird began giggling. Little Mouse joined in until they were both hugging again, laughing and gasping.

"Daughter," Wa-gi said quietly. Night Bird made herself grow calm to greet her uncle and aunt, but then she grabbed Little Mouse's hand. "Come see my village!" she said.

She showed her cousin everything. "There is the garbage pit." They hurried through the trees to a ring of buildings. "That's my chickee," she said, pointing to one of the huts near the fire. "And they're building a new chickee just for guests." They stopped to watch the men laying palm fronds on the roof. Through the open walls, they watched little children playing on the dirt floor.

"It will have a sleeping platform, don't worry. No snakes will slide in at night," Night Bird said. "You can sleep with me in my chickee."

"Here's the fire." She couldn't stop chattering, but Little Mouse didn't seem to mind. "That old dog always lies near the heat." The dog raised his ears and thumped his tail, but he didn't get up. "All my life, I've never heard him bark. Do you have dogs?"

"We did." There was so much sadness in Little Mouse's voice that Night Bird stopped chattering for a moment. They stood looking at the fire. It had burned there all year long. A year when Little Mouse had been lost and now found again, alive. What else happened to her in this year? Night Bird wondered. And what will happen by the new fire we light tomorrow?

A big iron pot of corn mush was boiling now at the center of the five logs. "Are you hungry?" Night Bird asked.

Little Mouse nodded and they helped themselves to ladles full of the sofkee mush and chunks of roast pumpkin. "I can't wait to taste the new corn tomorrow!" Night Bird said gaily.

"Out of the way, girls!" sang one of the men. He swung a deer down beside the fire and cut off a thin slice of its meat. The girls stood while he tossed the sliver onto the fire. Night Bird knew her mind should be full of thanks to the deer while its first meat was burned. Instead, she was thinking about her cousin.

"I have missed this," Little Mouse said.

Night Bird looked around the clearing. People wandered about, each doing his or her part to get ready for the feast. The fire roared with deer grease, and dogs sniffed closer to the heat. Chickens pecked in the sand by the corn grinder. Children sat passing the string game back and forth. An aunt from the Panther clan

stirred the sofkee. It was home. "It isn't like this in your village?"

"Don't you know?" Little Mouse looked at Night Bird. Her eyes were wide with surprise. "Doesn't anyone know?"

Know what? Night Bird wanted to ask. Watch and listen, she reminded herself. She turned at the sound of loud, angry voices.

"And you ran here to hide?" Da-ti stormed to the fireside. "You ran from the whites and came here? Now?"

"What were we to do?" Little Mouse's mother pleaded. "We escaped from the farm with other slaves, black ones."

"We didn't come straight here," Little Mouse's father said. "First we took our friends to the black village. Thank goodness they haven't moved it in the past few years. Our friends are safe now."

"But we aren't!" Night Bird had never seen her father so angry. "For years the blacks have been able to stay in their own chickees the way we taught them, farming their hummocks and raising their families. And there's only one reason!" He paused and stared at Little Mouse's parents.

A crowd had gathered around the fire. When Da-ti continued, his voice was even deeper. "They survived there because no one ever led the soldiers to their village. Or to ours."

"There is still a chance," another uncle said. "We

are so far out in the swamps. They won't follow . . . unless . . ."

"Unless a white person was killed in the escape."
Night Bird's father finished the sentence.

The village froze in silence. Every adult was staring
at Little Mouse's parents, waiting for the answer. Even
the children were quiet. Little Mouse's father glared
at the other Seminoles. Her mother looked at the
ground.

Night Bird looked at Little Mouse. Tears were running down her face. She put an arm around her cousin,
and Little Mouse began to cry.

"My father didn't mean to kill him! We had to get
away!" It all tumbled out between sobs. "It was so
awful. We just . . ." She was crying so much it was
hard to understand her now. ". . . we just wanted to
come home."

Night Bird hugged her. Around them, a terrible
silence stretched.

The Black Drink

"And you *did* come home!" Grandmother's voice rang out. "This is your home." She stared at the circle of villagers. "And every one of you would have done the same for your family. We need to make ready now. How many guns do we have? Frog clan, you handle defenses. Panthers, check the food. Are the canoes ready to load? The older children can check them." The villagers looked at one another and began to grumble.

"How much time do we have?" one finally said aloud.

"We've been traveling hard for a week," Little Mouse's mother said quietly. "And we did stop at the black village."

"We can still light the fire," one of the medicine men said. "And if the Giver of Breath is willing, we shall feast."

"And then we *all* must leave this hummock," the head of the Crab clan said. "Quickly. White soldiers will be coming."

What about the ribbon dance? Night Bird thought. And the day of fasting we must have before the feast? It won't be right!

"Remember *this!*" Grandmother said sharply. The fire crackled and sparks flew skyward. The Seminoles were silent. "With the first flame of the new year's fire, all of this will be forgotten. All the anger gone. All mistakes forgiven." She seemed to be daring someone to answer.

Night Bird knew that was how it was supposed to be. That was how it was every year. But it wasn't going to be easy this year.

"We need four days for the Green Corn ceremony. How are we going to do it all in one night?" Night Bird's question was on everyone's lips that afternoon.

"We'll leave it up to the medicine men," her mother told her. "They'll know what we need to do."

The medicine men—and Grandmother, Night Bird thought, following the old woman. She was every-

where, limping about and giving orders. She had a job in mind for everyone, it seemed. And she used the same cranky voice whether she was bossing toddlers or medicine men around.

The girls followed, helping anyone who needed it. "Watch and listen, Night Bird," Grandmother said. "And remember well. When you are head of the clan, you may have to do this someday."

Head of the clan. Night Bird hadn't thought about all that would mean. It had just sounded like fun before. But she might have to take charge like this.

She could never be as smart as Grandmother. All alone, the old woman had filled the village with calm. Around them, everyone was working to make the feast—and the leaving—happen in time. It made Night Bird feel proud to be an Otter.

Then Grandmother began saying things that made no sense at all. She reminded the women not to let their knives grow dull. She told the fire to hurry and roast the meat quicker. She even yelled at the sun to slow down in the sky. Before long, everyone was laughing at her, passing crazy-grandmother stories from job to job.

What is wrong with Grandmother? Night Bird wondered. She sat down beside her mother. Wa-gi handed an ear of corn to her. Night Bird began pulling off the tender new leaves, shucking the corn in time with her mother. New corn before the new fire, she thought.

Nothing was going in order. She was afraid. She was tired. And she was angry.

"Why is Grandmother saying such foolish things, Wa-gi? Trying to boss the fire and the sun around? People are laughing at her. At us."

"Yes, they are, Night Bird," Wa-gi said. "Listen to the village and tell me what you think." She handed Night Bird another ear of corn.

Night Bird listened. Stews bubbled and hissed over the fire. Women were singing. Children danced through the clearing, shaking the new rattles they'd made. Laughter was everywhere. So was the shrill voice of the "crazy old grandmother." Night Bird smiled and kept shucking corn.

By sunset, the feast was ready. It was all planned. If there was time, they would eat together after the new fire was lit at dawn. If they had to leave, each family could carry their share with them into hiding. The old fire was out and the clearing swept free of ashes. New logs were ready to be lit. Night Bird led the other children in spreading clean white sand throughout the village.

Tonight there would be a medicine dance. That was too important to skip. All men had to take the black drink before the new year—or before a battle. Now they had to be ready for either.

Night Bird and Little Mouse rushed to the chickee

when it was time to put on the new clothes. Her brothers and sisters ran along with them. "Do they always follow you around?" Little Mouse asked.

Night Bird hugged the older of her two little sisters. "I've been taking care of them a lot," she said. "Wa-gi has been sick, and besides, I'm in charge of them if something happens." *When* something happens, she thought. And it will probably happen tomorrow. She shivered.

Little Mouse helped Night Bird's younger brothers pull long, colorful shirts over their heads. She helped tie their sashes, too. Then she helped Night Bird's baby sister with her new skirt.

Night Bird dressed Amitee. Her favorite sister stood quietly, watching everything. Watching and listening, Night Bird realized. She gave Amitee a hug.

"Look, look, look!" the baby called in her squeaky little voice. She turned in circles until she was too dizzy to stand up. Little Mouse and Night Bird laughed together and then they were quiet.

"You must wear my skirt." Night Bird held it out to her cousin. Little Mouse shook her head no. She smoothed down the limp cloth of her strange dress. Is that a white person's dress? Night Bird wondered. How awful to have to wear white people's clothes to a Green Corn ceremony!

Little Mouse's eyes never left the bright band of colorful ribbons at the bottom of Night Bird's new clothing. "Go ahead," Night Bird said. "I can get another year's wear from this old skirt."

She tossed her new clothes to her cousin and squeaked, "Look, look, look!" just the way the baby had. Little Mouse backed out of the way as Night Bird began turning in circles. Little Mouse pulled off her old dress and put on the new skirt and top. Then both girls swung around in dizzy circles. It felt so good to be silly after all the fear.

"Ssssh!" the little ones hissed at them from the front of the chickee. "It's starting!" Over their heads, Night Bird and Little Mouse saw the medicine men bringing gourds full of the black drink into the clearing.

"What happens next?" Little Mouse asked quietly.

"You don't know?" Night Bird was surprised. How could anyone forget something so important?

"I never remember much unless it happens over and over," Little Mouse whispered.

"You *do* remember songs?"

"If I sing them again and again. Even then I sometimes forget. Why?"

"How about stories?"

"Oh, I can remember stories just fine. Not every little word, like some people do. I tell them in my own way. And sometimes I change them. It's fun."

Night Bird could not imagine changing the old stories. The words were the stories—how they sounded, how they felt. How could you ever remember a ceremony, with all the dances and chants, if you couldn't hold a story in your mind? How could you be an Otter without a memory?

"Do you see our mothers?" she whispered. Little Mouse pointed across the moonlit clearing to where the women were sitting silently in the shadows under the trees. They all had pulled their shawls tight around their shoulders.

Night Bird took Little Mouse's hand and led her to the front of the chickee. They sat, leaning against a log. Night Bird explained the ceremony to all the children. She told of the dark-colored drink and its magic. How bad it was supposed to taste. How it cleaned out a man and made him pure and strong again.

"I know that," Amitee said.

"You don't know it all yet. Listen and watch." Night Bird patted her sister on the shoulder. The men drank in silence, then danced and danced again. Medicine bundles wrapped in leather lay in a row on the far side of the fire circle. No one but the medicine men knew what was inside the holy bundles. No one but a medicine man would dare use their power. Night Bird thought she could see the medicine bundles glowing. But perhaps it was the moonlight.

Then the men were all dancing.

The moonlight gleamed on shaven heads. The air was filled with drumming and chants. One by one, the men left the circle while the drink worked its magic.

The girls could hear the dancers throwing up beyond the trees.

"How awful," Little Mouse whispered.

How wonderful, Night Bird thought. She tried to imagine being able to throw away every bit of worry and anger that burned in her own stomach. But the black drink was only for men. She followed along with the chant, mouthing every word and swaying gently in the darkness.

Drums beat without end: now slow, now fast. One by one, the younger children fell asleep. Night Bird moved them into the center of the chickee and tossed blankets over them. Soon only she and Little Mouse were awake to watch. And then her cousin's breathing slowed and deepened.

Night Bird covered her gently. Then she crept out and took her place with the women of the Otter clan.

Run and Hide!

Night Bird couldn't breathe. She struggled to wake up from her dream. A horrid dream. A hand covered her mouth and squeezed. She tried to wriggle free. End, she told the dream. She fought for a breath. No air. There was no air!

"You must run, daughter." It was her mother's voice, close to her ear. "Run and hide with the little ones."

Night Bird's eyes popped open. She blinked hard. Wa-gi's head was just a shadow against the dark sky. Night Bird nodded. Her mother took her hand off Night Bird's mouth and let her breathe.

"Take Little Mouse. Hide in the hole under the bank. Wait for me there." And her mother disappeared into the darkness.

Night Bird rolled off her sleeping blanket. Quick shadows hurried past the chickee, whispering softly. She could hear the sounds of bare feet padding about. A quiet cough. A jingle as some man put on his breast-plate—her father? The sound of water spilled gently against the ground.

Suddenly a baby's cry sliced into the night. Just as suddenly, the cry was cut off.

Night Bird held her breath. Around her, she could feel the village, frozen, waiting. All she could hear was the humming of mosquitoes and the beating of her own heart.

The darkness lifted slowly. Now she could pick out shapes. Fathers. Mothers. Children. All moving more slowly, more quietly than before. A night heron croaked as it flew over, heading for its hummock and safety.

Run and hide. Night Bird knew what she had to do. She only wished she knew why. Could the soldiers have gotten here already?

She moved carefully to Amitee's side. Would her sister be scared? Would she, too, cry out? Night Bird brushed the bangs from the little one's forehead and made her hand ready to cover her mouth if she cried.

"Sister," she whispered. Dark eyes opened and met hers in the dim twilight. No screaming. They'd gone through the plans together—and this child remembered well.

The boys awakened quietly, too. Even the littlest sister was quiet. Night Bird was filled with love for this family. Don't let anything happen to them, she pleaded silently. Together they crept to the corner where Little Mouse slept. "Come, cousin." Night Bird shook the girl's shoulder.

Little Mouse pushed her hand away and rolled over. "Not now," she grumbled. Night Bird shook her again. "Why do we have to go?"

Why won't she just do what needs to be done? Night Bird wondered. And be quiet about it!

She put her fingers to Little Mouse's lips, but she couldn't quiet her cousin's nervous chatter. "It's the soldiers, isn't it?" Little Mouse said. "They've come for me. I know it. Do they have dogs?"

A gunshot blasted through the silence. Night Bird slid off the chickee platform and lifted her brothers and sisters down carefully. She didn't look back, but she heard Little Mouse's footsteps following her. She ran through the trees, past the rubbish pit, right to the edge of the hummock and over the steep bank.

Amitee helped her pull aside the grasses from the opening of the hiding place. Little Mouse stood, panting, behind her. Night Bird pointed silently into the hole. Little Mouse shook her head no. Amitee crawled right in. She threw a snake out into the water and they all jumped at the noise of its splash.

The boys crawled in. Night Bird pointed again at her cousin and then to the hole. Little Mouse shook her head and pointed up toward the villlage.

No! Night Bird wanted to shout. All she could do was watch as Little Mouse climbed back up the slope.

Another gunshot split the silence and Night Bird dove into the hole. It was a tight fit for the five of them. But Little Mouse would have fit inside, too, Night Bird thought. The hole smelled of dampness, of worms, and of rot. A safe smell. She was pulling the grasses back over the opening when the yelling started.

"Seminoles!" a strange voice called. "Come out! We are friends. Don't shoot!" A gun blast was the only answer Night Bird heard. Was it a Seminole gun or a white soldier's? Where had Wa-gi gone? Da-ti? Night Bird hugged the little ones close.

A canoe slid into view through the curtain of grasses covering their hole. A white man looked at the bank. Night Bird blinked. He had hair everywhere! She looked closer. He wasn't dressed like a soldier. At least not like the soldiers in the stories Night Bird had heard. As the canoe slid past Night Bird gasped. There was a *Seminole* poling the boat through the water!

He was the one doing all the yelling. "I know you can all hear me. Let me talk to you." The canoe swung in toward the hiding hole. "Hold your fire."

Night Bird pulled the little ones back from the open- ing and held them tighter still. The splash of men's

feet hitting the water filled the hole. Night Bird closed her eyes. Footsteps pounded right up the bank beside her head. More sounds floated down from over the bank. Footsteps. Another gunshot. Curses. And then the screaming began.

Night Bird froze. She knew that voice. It was Little Mouse's!

Go—or Stay?

The screaming went on and on. Then there was a smacking sound. A heavy thud. And Little Mouse's screams stopped.

"I've got her!" the voice called out. It had to be the Seminole. "You shoot me and you've shot the girl! Now let's talk!"

Little Mouse started crying again, softly this time. Night Bird's teeth were chattering. She put her fingers between her teeth to stop the noise.

The talking went on and on. Night Bird couldn't hear much of it, but the Seminole kept repeating a strange word—"Oklahoma." It had to be a white word.

And he kept saying "peace." All the while, Little Mouse sobbed quietly.

Footsteps again, scrambling, sliding down the bank and into the swamp nearby. No one in the hole breathed.

A shadow passed over the entrance. Night Bird slid forward to watch the men as they splashed back toward the canoe. One was Seminole and one was white. She stared. She couldn't help it. She had stopped believing that horrible things would happen to her if she looked at a white person. Didn't her own father trade skins with them for guns and cloth, beads and iron pots? Horrible things had never happened to him.

The white man had a small head, but it was very hairy. And there was hair all over his face. She wrinkled her nose. It looked dirty. He wore leather on his feet and tight pants up to his waist. How bad that must feel, she thought.

"We leave for Oklahoma in two weeks!" the Seminole man shouted to the person who was on the bank over Night Bird's head. "You can have your own land there. No more fighting. Ever. Think about it!" And then they were gone.

Night Bird thought about it. She thought about it until Wa-gi called her out of the hole. She thought about it as she made her brothers and sisters do their morning washing. She was still thinking about it as she joined the other villagers by the four cold logs waiting for fire.

The fire should have been lit at dawn, but they couldn't wait until sunrise tomorrow. Everything was in place now. One log pointing in each of the four sacred directions. Medicine bundles next to the men. A heap of fine grasses ready to be lit. It all looked right—but it didn't sound right.

The people were arguing.

"We should go!"

"Never!"

Husbands were fighting with their wives. Their children stood in shocked silence or cried in fear.

"How can we trust him?"

"You know who he was. That is a good man."

"But he makes deals with the soldiers. And they never keep their word."

Sister argued with sister, father with son. "How far is this Oklahoma?"

"I'll never go!"

Wa-gi and Da-ti were standing in silence. They wouldn't look at her. They wouldn't look at each other, either. Night Bird stood by them a moment, then walked away from their anger.

She found Little Mouse. Her cousin's eye was going to be black and blue. They had hit her in the eye! "Does it hurt?" she asked. Little Mouse shook her head no and blinked hard. Night Bird took her hand and held it tightly.

Grandmother limped to the center of the crossed logs. The crowd hushed. "Light it," she said. Her voice was calm and quiet. "Light it. This is a new year. We have hours to choose who will stay in the swamps and who will go to this Oklahoma place." This was not the crazy old woman from yesterday. This woman stood tall in a fine new skirt. She was wearing more beads around her neck than anyone else in the village.

"We will *not* begin a year in anger," she said to the medicine man who'd been fighting with his wife.

The Fire Maker faced east, where the sun had already risen, and struck the flint. The spark fell into the dry grass. First there was a tiny curl of smoke, then a flicker of flame. The new year had begun.

The songs were not sung. No one danced the dances. There was none of the joy that the new harvest and a new year should bring.

"All the Otters will feast with me," Grandmother said as soon as the flames began to spread. Night Bird helped to gather her clan's part of the feast. Her feet moved slowly. There would be no dancing this year.

Night Bird and Little Mouse crowded under the thatched roof of one chickee with their families. Night Bird looked at Grandmother. The old woman's eyes looked sad and tired and distant. What is she dreaming of now? Night Bird wondered. The old days when there were a hundred Otters? Or was she asking herself how many would be left tomorrow?

"This is the chance I've always wanted for my

children," Wa-gi said. Night Bird could tell she was trying hard to keep her voice quiet.

"But it may be dangerous," Da-ti said.

"Living here is dangerous," Night Bird's mother said. "Those white men didn't know about the escape yet." She looked at Little Mouse's parents. "Or about the killing. Others will come. And they *will* know."

Grandmother looked from one daughter to the other. "And what do you want, dear?" she asked Little Mouse's mother.

"I am finally home after a year of slavery. I won't go anywhere else. I won't." She looked at Wa-gi with tears running down her cheeks. "I will miss you, sister." They hugged long and hard.

"That is right," Grandmother said. Everyone turned to her in surprise. "This way there will be Otters here to remember the ceremonies and Otters to carry them to the Oklahoma place, too," she explained. "But what of the girls?"

"They'll stay with us," both mothers said at once.

"They are old enough to make that choice for themselves," Grandmother said. Little Mouse and Night Bird stared at each other, speechless.

"No," Night Bird's father said. "I want my wife, my daughter, and you to come with us to Oklahoma."

"It is not your choice," Grandmother said. "This is clan business. A clan follows the women. And," she added, "I will be staying here. Have some stew."

Throughout the rest of the meal, each woman tried to get her daughter to choose to stay—or to go—with her. Little Mouse promised she'd stay with her mother forever.

Night Bird was too shocked to think clearly. And she had to. This was so important.

She ate. She passed food to her brothers. She held a water gourd for her baby sister. She watched Amitee break a piece of roast pumpkin in two so both boys got the same share. Then Night Bird helped to clean up. Still she couldn't think. Go or stay? It was too important. Quiet, she thought. I must think in quiet.

"Little Mouse and Night Bird," Grandmother said, "you will come with me now to collect some herbs." Both sets of parents started to argue. "I need some for my pain and I expect Little Mouse could use some for that black eye." Little Mouse smiled and nodded. "My elder daughter will need some for her trip," Grandmother added. "And for having a baby." Night Bird looked quickly at her mother.

Wa-gi smiled at her. "You'd have known it soon," she said.

"I'll pole the canoe for you," Night Bird told Grandmother. She stood to help the old woman to her feet.

"Night Bird?" Wa-gi said.

Night Bird stopped for a moment. "I do hope it is a girl," she said.

Her brothers looked at her in surprise. "Girls grow up, marry, and have more babies for the Otter clan," she reminded them. "Your children will belong to your wives' clans. They'll be important, too, but we need more Otters."

Then she and Little Mouse walked Grandmother to the canoe, one girl holding each arm.

Oklahoma?

"Wait!" Night Bird called to Little Mouse. "Look first." She stood on the bank above the canoe, searching the water. "No alligators," she said after a moment. "It's safe." Perhaps Little Mouse had never known a child to be eaten, she thought.

Little Mouse sat in the front of the canoe, Grandmother in the middle. Night Bird stood in the back and held the pole. As long as she could remember, she had loved poling. She smiled, thinking how tiny she—and the stick—had been at first. Now she used a tall pole. She felt it settle deep into the mud, then hit firm ground. She pushed off the bank toward the burying hummock.

"That's where we'll find what we need," Grandmother had said.

All three were silent as the canoe eased through the channel. But there was only one thing on all three minds—and each of them knew it. Oklahoma.

Night Bird tried to remember everything they'd been told about the distant place. Oklahoma was dry. But there must be some water because it go so cold there that water froze hard. The farmland was good and they could own their own farm. Why do you need to own land? she wondered. And they said you would never have to fight again. If you could believe the white men.

More facts: Wa-gi and Da-ti were going to Oklahoma. They would take care of her if she went with them. She would miss them so much if she stayed in the Everglades without them. But they had other children, and Wa-gi was carrying another baby. Night Bird wasn't needed in Oklahoma.

Grandmother was not going. Night Bird stared at the old woman, sitting tall and proud in the canoe. The breeze stirred a few loose gray hairs and she pushed them firmly back into place. Such a strong ruler, Night Bird thought. But wise enough to play the fool when needed. Full of memories. Full of pain.

She wanted to protect the old woman, but she wasn't really needed here, either. Little Mouse and her parents would take care of Grandmother. Only if she lets them, Night Bird thought with a smile.

Where was she needed?

She let her mind go empty as she poled on and on into the warmth of the Everglades. Sawgrass whispered against the bottom of the canoe. Frogs chirped. Everywhere the *pop-smack* of feeding fish broke the surface of the water. The hum of mosquitoes. The buzzing of dragonfly wings. And the soft croaking of night herons on the nest. Home sounds. Night Bird took a deep breath. She needed the special kind of quiet the Everglades gave her.

And the sky! Night Bird looked up into endless blue. Already, thunderclouds were growing at the edges of the sky. All afternoon they would parade past, tall and powerful. And they'd be gone by nightfall. Then the stars! Would there be skies like this in Oklahoma? There was no one to ask. As much as she needed them, the Everglades did not need her. And neither did the sky.

Where *was* she needed, then?

Watch and listen. The thought filled her mind as the canoe slid onto land. Grandmother stepped out and nearly fell on her bad foot. Little Mouse got out to help. Night Bird pushed and pulled the canoe firmly onto the mud.

"Do you girls know what to look for?" Grandmother asked.

"Herbs for teas. Herbs to take the sting from wounds.

Roots to grind for healing," Night Bird said, pointing to plants growing right in front of them on the bank. "Is anything else ready just now?"

Little Mouse looked amazed. Grandmother just laughed. "Your mother has taught you well, Night Bird. But yes, there is another plant. To make child-birth easier. Follow me."

As they walked around the edge of the hummock Grandmother pointed out a dozen herbs that Night Bird did not know. Grandmother seemed to have a use for every plant on the island. When she caught Night Bird's look of wonder, she chuckled. "Remember what I told you. I'm not smart. I'm just old. And," she added, "I don't let myself forget."

They walked around the island again, and Grandmother quizzed them on the plants they'd passed the first time. Night Bird remembered most of it, but Little Mouse was confused. "I'm out of practice," she said. "We never did this when we were"—her voice changed—"slaves."

Night Bird reached for Little Mouse's hand. Her cousin was staring out over the swamps. Her face looked so sad. What was she remembering?

"Grandmother, do you have time to show us more?" Night Bird asked. "We'll never forget," she promised.

"I want to get back to help my parents pack," said Little Mouse. "They say there are plenty of hiding places left in the Everglades. You *are* going to go to Oklahoma with your folks, aren't you, Night Bird?"

"Do you want me to go?" Night Bird asked.

"No!" Little Mouse sounded shocked. "Of course I want you to stay here with us. I think I could learn a lot from you. Mostly we could have fun." She grinned, then shook her head. Night Bird remembered their giggling dance with Little Mouse in the new skirt.

"But Night Bird," Little Mouse asked, "how can you even think about letting your parents go without you?"

"I don't know." Tears filled Night Bird's eyes. She thought about her father, strong in his breastplate. Her mother, warm and wise. The new baby coming. She thought about her little brothers and sisters— especially Amitee. The smart one. The one who would remember.

And then she knew who needed her.

"I'm ready," she said to Grandmother.

The Race

Half of the canoes were already gone when Night Bird poled her boat to the hummock. Some families were at the shore, packing. Others were carrying bundles down from the village. The Seminoles were very, very quiet.

They should be hurrying, Night Bird thought. They should be racing to safety. But everyone was moving slowly. And they all looked so tired.

Little Mouse suddenly stood up. She shaded her eyes and looked at the people on the shore. "Do you see my parents?" she asked Night Bird. The boat rocked.

"Sit down!" Night Bird and Grandmother said together.

Little Mouse sat. Her mouth opened, then closed. She looked as if she might cry. "They wouldn't leave me," she finally said. Then she added, "Would they?"

Night Bird poled faster. She could see her own parents on the bank. Where *were* Little Mouse's parents?

Grandmother began to chuckle. Night Bird turned to look where the old woman was pointing. Another canoe was following them. In it were Little Mouse's parents.

"Turn around!" Little Mouse told Night Bird when she saw them. "Please."

The canoe was already brushing the bottom mud. "I can't turn it now," Night Bird said.

"I want my mother." Little Mouse's eyes were full of tears. A man on the shore shook his head at her. How does it look, Night Bird thought, an eleven-year-old crying for her mother—an Otter—and in front of all these people? They would all remember it. She didn't know what to do for her cousin.

Grandmother did.

"Give me the pole," she whispered, and stood up. "Lean against my bad leg." Night Bird stepped closer and sat down. Grandmother gave a great push with the pole, and the canoe began to glide backward.

"What?" the man on shore yelled. Other villagers turned to look.

Grandmother was poling the canoe faster and faster,

backward toward Little Mouse's parents. People on shore began to laugh. "Wrong way, old woman!" one called. The laughter sounded good.

How can she be so fast? Night Bird wondered. When she felt the old lady's leg quivering through her skirt, Night Bird knew it wasn't easy for her. She began to push against her grandmother's leg in time with the poling.

Soon the canoes met. Both boats rocked as Little Mouse stepped over into her parents' canoe. "Mother!" she cried. "Father!" And the three stood hugging.

Grandmother looked down at Night Bird. She grinned, planted the pole into the mud, and cried aloud, "Let's race!"

Before Little Mouse's father could get out of the hug, Grandmother and Night Bird were off. The old woman was as good with a pole as any man Night Bird had ever seen. And with her pushing against Grandmother, the canoe flew across the water.

The villagers began to cheer. Night Bird looked back. The other canoe was gaining. "Hurry!" she said.

The canoes touched the shore together. Children were cheering and their parents were laughing. One man patted Little Mouse's father on the head. Another pretended to feel Grandmother's strong arms. There were no more sad faces in the village.

Another story to remember, Night Bird told herself. She knew this story would be told over fires in Oklahoma as well as fires here in the swamps. And where else? she wondered. Where do stories end?

Both girls stood with their families by the new fire. Tonight there should have been feasting, Night Bird thought as she looked into the blaze. And the ribbon dance. And a few—a very few—of the girls would get a string of beads to wear forever. If they were lucky and if their growth had pleased their parents.

But by tonight, this camp would be empty, the fire dead. No feast, no dancing, no beads.

"Where are my things?" she asked Wa-gi.

"They're packed with ours," her mother said. "The family is ready to go."

"I'll need my things here." Night Bird turned quickly to walk to the chickee. And to hide her tears.

"Here?" Her mother's voice sounded shocked and hurt. "You're staying here?" This was not going to be easy, Night Bird knew. "Who will help with the babies? Who will I teach?" She followed Night Bird, tossing questions at her back, not waiting for answers. "When would I see you again?"

Night Bird prayed that they would get to the chickee before she had to answer. "You're doing it just so you can be near Little Mouse, aren't you?" Wa-gi said. Anger filled her voice.

"No!" It was easy to be honest about that question.

"Then you are staying to be with my mother?" Wa-gi's voice softened. Night Bird could almost say yes, for this was partly true. But only partly.

She climbed onto the platform in the chickee. Her

mother pulled herself up, too, and crawled back to the pile of bedding where Night Bird was searching for her belongings.

"You really won't go to Oklahoma for me?"

Night Bird shook her head. She wouldn't turn until she could control the sobs that filled her throat.

Finally she took a deep breath and looked at her mother. "I'm staying here because of Amitee," she said.

"Amitee?"

"Teach *her*, Wa-gi. Show *her*. She will be a wonderful head for the clan in Oklahoma."

Wa-gi was silent. Then she nodded. "I never saw that," she said. There was wonder in her voice. "Little Amitee."

"With what I know, and with what Grandmother can teach me," Night Bird said, "I can lead the Otters. My daughters—and their daughters after them—will be a strong clan. Here. In the Everglades." And now the sobs broke through. "But I will miss you so."

Wa-gi hugged her tightly and helped Night Bird pull her things out of the family's pack. She carried the little bundle to the clearing. There, she stopped.

"She's *not* staying behind," Night Bird's father said.

"She is," said Wa-gi quietly. "She is doing it for the clan." She took a full handful of necklaces off her own neck and settled them over Night Bird's head.

And Grandmother did the same.

In 1820, there were 5,000 Seminole Indians living in the Southeast. Just 38 years later, there were fewer than 200 left hiding in the Everglades. What happened to them all?

United States soldiers killed many Seminole Indians in wars that began in 1835. How many? Nobody bothered to keep a record. Other Seminoles were taken to work as slaves on Southern farms. Many more of these Native Americans were forced or bribed, tricked or talked into moving to Oklahoma. The few left in Florida at the end of the wars in 1858 went into hiding deep in the Everglades.

What was it all about? Land, at first. White settlers pushed the Indians farther and farther south, off good farmland and into the swamps. For a long time, the Indians had protected black slaves who escaped from Southern farms. They took them into their own villages and families or taught them how to live free in the Everglades. This made the farmers and the government angry enough to want to get every Seminole out of the South, one way or another. They took them as slaves. They shipped them to Oklahoma. They killed them. Sometimes the Indians fought back. Mostly they fled deeper into the Everglades.

Nearly all the Seminoles were gone when the wars were finally called off in 1858. The government had other things on its mind. Another war was begin-ning—the Civil War, a war between the states that would end all slavery in the United States.

Night Bird and the clans in this book never existed, but the real-life Seminoles who stayed in hiding in Florida and those who survived the march to Oklahoma remembered the long wars. But they also remembered the dances, the ceremonies, and the stories of their Seminole clans. They taught them to their children, and to their children's children.

Today there are about 3,000 Seminoles living in Oklahoma. There are more than 2,000 Seminoles in Florida, split into two separate tribes. Most live in modern houses with TVs and stoves. A few in Florida still live in old-style chickees, tell stories at night, and cook on open fires.

At the Green Corn ceremony, they celebrate the new harvest and put an end to the wrongs of the past year. At powwows that you can visit, Seminole girls in new skirts still dance the ancient ribbon dance.

I visited the Florida Seminoles to learn more about them for this book. I spent time in tribal and government offices and libraries and looked at museum exhibits. I asked questions everywhere I went, but I also took the time to watch and listen, learning in the old Seminole way.

K.V.K.